# LIVE BAIT

# LIVE BAIT

## Richard Laymon

**FEARON/JANUS/QUERCUS**
Belmont, California

Simon & Schuster Education Group

## FASTBACK® HORROR BOOKS

Cover photographer: Richard Hutchings

ISBN 0-8224-3770-8

Printed in the United States of America.

2. 14 13 12 11 10 9 8 7 6 5
DE

Nora rubbed her face, trying to keep awake as she drove through the night. A few miles back, she had passed a diner. The gloomy look of the place had put her off. Now she wished that she had stopped there for a cup of coffee.

Since leaving it behind, she'd come upon no more restaurants, gas stations, or roadside businesses of any kind. She saw a few cabins off among the trees. A while ago, a car had passed, heading in the other direction.

If she had known the road was going to be this deserted, she would have spent the night at a motel in Hayward. Then she could have finished the drive to Beth's place in the morning.

Well, she ought to reach her friend's cabin in another hour or so. She could last that long. It was going to be great seeing Beth again after all these months, and great going out on the lake in the new powerboat tomorrow.

Yawning, she leaned forward to turn up the radio. As she twisted the knob, she steered around a curve. Her headlights swept onto a tree limb on the road just ahead. In an instant, she decided not to try swerving around it. There was not enough time. Besides, the branch didn't look very large.

Her front tires bumped over it. She heard a crackle of leafy branches, then scraping sounds as the limb was dragged along under the car. A few moments later, the rear tires thumped over it. She checked the rearview mirror. In the red glow of her taillights, she glimpsed the limb behind her, still stretched across the lane.

*For someone else to hit.*

With a sigh, Nora stepped on the brake. She eased her car to the side of the road, and stopped. After turning on the emergency flashers, she climbed out.

It felt good to stand up after sitting so

long behind the wheel. She stretched, enjoying the way her straining muscles felt, and then walked toward the tree limb.

The road was dark except for a few patches of moonlight. Her sneakers made quiet sounds on the pavement. At first, the night seemed silent. Then she noticed the forest sounds. She heard leaves stirring in the breeze, the squawk and twitter of birds, the lonely hoot of an owl. Crickets and frogs added their noises to the night, and so did a mosquito humming near Nora's ear.

Crouching, she wrapped her hands around the limb's trunk near its broken end. She walked backwards, dragging it off the road. Her hands felt gritty. She wiped them on the legs of her jeans, and walked toward the red, blinking lights of her car.

*Your good deed for the day*, she thought.

Then she saw that her car looked lopsided.

She rushed toward it, but stopped suddenly when she realized what was wrong. She felt as if she'd been punched in the stomach. She bent over, grabbed her knees and groaned.

*No*, she thought. *Not here, in the middle of nowhere. Not now, in the middle of the night. It can't be true.*

But it was true.

She lifted her head and stared at the left side of her car. The front and rear tires looked as if they'd been mashed against the pavement.

*Two flats.*

*Only one spare in the trunk.*

Nora let out a trembling breath and thought, *Why me?*

$S$he knew there was no place to get help on the stretch of road she had just traveled. Ahead, the road curved through the woods. If she hiked in that direction, she might find a gas station or an all-night diner with a telephone.

Her only other choice was to stay with the car and hope that someone would come along, sooner or later, and give her a lift. She didn't like that idea. She had never been one to depend upon others for help. She preferred to take action on her own. Besides, as deserted as the area seemed, she might spend the whole night waiting. Beth was expecting her to show up tonight. If she didn't, her friend would be frantic with worry.

Nora locked the car and started to walk. As she rounded the bend, she spotted a cabin through the trees. Lights glowed from its windows.

She stared up the moon-splashed road. It ran straight as an arrow for a long distance, with nothing along the way except dark woods. She might walk miles, only to find herself far from the car and no closer to help.

The cabin, at least, ought to have a

telephone. Whoever lived there surely wouldn't mind letting her use it. After all, this was an emergency.

She stepped off the road and headed through trees toward the cabin. Twigs and dead leaves crunched under her feet.

From the cabin, she thought she could call Beth and tell her what happened. Maybe Beth could drive out and meet her. They could change the tires using the spares from both cars and soon be on their way.

That idea lifted Nora's spirits. She walked faster. The cabin looked rundown. Behind it, a glowing light revealed a dock. She glimpsed a motorboat, and a trail of moonlight on a lake. Wondering which lake this might be, she tried to recall her map. Maybe Marvel or Arkham. She wasn't sure. But the people in the cabin would know, so she could tell Beth where to find her.

Cutting across the overgrown yard, she looked again at the windows. The curtains were shut. She climbed three stairs to the porch, and stopped in front of the door. Gently, she rapped on it.

A few seconds passed. She was about to knock again when the porch light came on. She took a quick step backwards, and brushed a mosquito off her cheek. Then the door swung open.

A man glanced out at her. Leaning through the doorway, he looked to each side. He was well over six feet tall, with thick hairy arms. The sleeves had been cut from his faded blue shirt. The front of the shirt was spotted with paints of many colors. It hung loose over the top of his knee-length shorts. His feet were bare.

"What can I do for you?" he asked. His voice sounded high and clear, not the low rumble Nora expected from a man his size.

"I'm sorry to bother you," she said, "but I ran into some car trouble. I was wondering if you might have a phone I could use."

He flung back his head to swing a flap of black hair away from his eyes. "Sure," he said. "Come on in."

He stepped aside, and Nora entered the cabin. The air smelled of paint. She stared at the walls. They were covered with framed canvases. She got a sick feeling in her stomach as she looked from one painting to another.

She turned around.

The man locked the door.

"What's wrong?" he asked.

Nora shook her head.

He smiled. "My paintings, I bet. They do upset some people. On the other hand, I have customers who pay top dollar for my work. They sell like hotcakes at the art fairs." He held out a hand to Nora. "I'm Steve," he said.

She shook his hand. "Nora," she told him.

"Nice to meet you. I don't get many callers way out here in the boondocks."

Nora nodded. Steve's friendly manner calmed her a little.

"Folks in these parts stay clear. They don't care much for artists, anyway. And some of them seem to think I must be a nut to paint this kind of stuff."

Nora glanced at a nearby oil of a woman in flames. The painting beside it showed a hanged man, his tongue drooping out, his neck stretched. She looked back at Steve. "I can see why," she said, trying to smile. "They *are* pretty horrible."

He chuckled softly. "Everyone to his own taste. How would you like to see my masterpiece? It's not quite finished yet, but . . ."

"Could I use the phone first?" Nora asked.

"Sure. Right over there." He pointed at a telephone resting on a table near the couch.

"Thank you. I'll be glad to pay."

"Don't think of it."

Thanking him again, she stepped over to the phone. She lifted its receiver off the cradle, and listened for the dial tone. There was none. She picked up the plastic base. A foot of cord dangled from it. Steve, behind her, started to laugh. She whirled around and threw the phone at his head.

As he ducked, she dashed past him. She flung herself against the door, grabbed the knob, twisted it and tugged. The door stayed shut.

"You can't get out," Steve said in a cheerful voice. "Face it, you're caught. Nobody ever gets away from tricky Steve."

Nora turned to him.

He grinned and rubbed his chin.

"What do you want?" she asked. Her voice came out in a whisper.

"I've got what I want—you."

"Why?"

"I am an artist. An artist needs a model." He waved a hand toward the walls of gory paintings. "Do you think I make up such things? Do you think I shut my eyes and *pretend*? No no, Steve doesn't work that way. Steve is a great artist. He works from life."

Nora shook her head. Her legs felt

weak, and she leaned against the door for
support.

Steve, a grin still baring his upper
teeth, pointed at the painting of the
woman in flames. "This was Eleanor. She
dropped in—oh, back in March. She had
car trouble, just like you. Flat tires. It
seems she ran over a branch in the road.
Maybe you ran over the same branch. Did
you notice the nails in it?"

"You're crazy," Nora gasped.

He wiggled his black eyebrows. "More
than likely." He chuckled. "Mad as a hat-
ter. Quite insane. That's why I'm a great
artist. It gives me my own slant on life . . .
and death."

Nora scanned the walls. She saw a
painting of a woman drowned in a tub,

hair floating, and eyes staring up through the water. Another showed a young man with a slashed throat, the wound looking like a big red grin. Nora guessed there were nine or ten canvases in all. She looked at Steve. "You . . . you *killed* these people?"

He nodded. "They were my models."

"And I'm your next model."

"Did I say that?"

"Didn't you?"

"I don't think so. No, you're not to be my model. I already have my model. Would you like to see? This is the master-piece I mentioned earlier." Grabbing Nora's arm, he yanked her forward. He held on tightly, leading her across the room. Propped on an easel near the far corner was a shrouded canvas larger than most of the others—a yard high and four feet across.

"Some artists won't show a work until it's done. But I expect to finish it tonight, and you will play a key part in it. You should be proud."

He pulled the cloth away from the painting.

Nora stared.

"Neat, huh?"

Nora answered with a groan.

"I call it *The Beast of Arkham Lake*."

The painting showed a lake at night. On the water's surface floated a giant *thing*, a twisted form of gray flesh, glistening and slimy in the moonlight. High above it, wrapped in a thick tentacle, was a man. His mouth gaped in a silent scream. Nora shuddered as she gazed at the head of the beast. It looked almost human, but much too large. It was tilted back, its tongue reaching through rows of dripping teeth toward the man. Its eyes were milky blobs.

"Isn't it great?" Steve asked. "You can't imagine how much work I've put into it. Weeks and weeks. I discovered my friend purely by accident, of course. I had no idea such a creature might exist, much less live in my own backyard, so to speak. I was out on the lake working on a painting I was going to call *Floating Corpse*, when up pops my model into the air. I tell you, I was more than a little surprised.

I'm not easily shocked, but I took one look at that thing waving him in its tentacles, and I almost lost my nerve. Luckily, it didn't seem much interested in me. It hung around for . . . oh, five minutes or so while it gobbled him up . . . and that gave me time to make a few sketches.

"After that night, I kept taking my boat out on the lake. But it just wouldn't show itself unless I brought along a snack for it. That's why the painting has taken so long. After all, my branch in the road doesn't always do the trick. It's been two months, and you're only the eighth person to drop in. Of course, sometimes there are passengers. I can handle a party of two, but any more than that gets risky, so I don't fool with them."

Steve laughed. "Can't be too careful,

you know," he said. "You can't be too patient, either. Not when you're creating a masterpiece to live through the ages. I knew that, sooner or later, someone else would turn up. And I was right. Here you are."

Smiling, he squeezed Nora's arm. It was already numb from his tight grip.

"Do you see what's wrong with the painting?"

She didn't try to answer.

"The eyes. I've saved them for last. Ask any artist, the eyes are the most important part of any portrait. You have to get them just right to capture the soul of your subject and really bring it to life. I'll finish the eyes tonight, though. With *you* as bait, Nora."

He jerked her backwards and tripped her. As she fell, the back of her head slammed against the floor.

When Nora came to, she was lying on her back. The floor seemed to be lifting and rolling gently under her. She tried to move, but something was wrapped around her hands and feet.

Opening her eyes, she saw that she was on the deck of a motorboat. Her head was near the stern. Her hands and feet were tied with rope. As she struggled to sit up, she heard footsteps nearby.

Steve, the big painting in his arms,

stepped onto the gunnel. His weight made the boat tip for an instant before he jumped down to the deck. "Hope I haven't kept you waiting," he said.

"You can't do this," she said.

"Art demands sacrifices, my dear. Madness, patience and sacrifice, the three keys to greatness." He carried his painting to an easel in the middle of the deck. The three legs of the easel, Nora saw, were bolted down to keep it upright while the boat was in motion. Carefully, Steve clamped the canvas in place. He wiggled it to make sure it wouldn't fall from the easel.

Then he untied the mooring lines and stepped to the controls. A moment later, the twin outboard motors rumbled to life.

The boat glided forward, then slowly gained speed.

Steve, hunched over the wheel, had his back to Nora. She raised her tied hands to her mouth and bit into the rope, tugging at the knot with her teeth. Soon, it loosened. She shook her head and got it open, only to find another knot. And there was still another one beneath that. If she had ten minutes, she might be able to free herself.

The thunder of the motors faded to a quiet putter. The boat slowed, its prow easing down toward the water.

Nora's teeth tore at the knot, but she couldn't budge it. She tried to twist her hands and yank them free. The rope cut into her wrists. It was much too tight.

The motors went silent. "Almost time," Steve said over his shoulder. Then he stepped onto the foredeck to drop anchor.

Nora brought her knees up to her chin.

The anchor made a thudding splash as it hit the water.

She pushed with her feet. Her back scraped against the side of the boat as she raised herself. With a final thrust, she was standing.

"Hey," Steve called, "you're too eager." He laughed as he walked toward her. "We're not ready yet. I have to get the floodlights on and my palette . . ."

He made a sudden dash for Nora as she threw herself forward. Her shoulder crashed against the painting, knocking it over the side and splintering the wooden legs of the easel.

"No!" Steve yelled. He shoved Nora aside. As she fell to the deck, she saw him reach out over the water, trying to grab the canvas. He caught a corner of it. His cry of delight turned to a shriek as the weight of the painting made him lose his balance. His knees bumped against the gunnel. His feet flew into the air. Then he was gone.

His splash sent a cool spray of water over the side of the boat onto Nora. Struggling to her knees, she looked down at the lake.

Moonlit ripples spread across the surface in growing circles.

Then Steve burst from the water. He held the painting and broken easel overhead as he kicked toward the sky, screaming. Coiled around his waist like a huge snake was a tentacle of his model—the beast of Arkham Lake.

Nora slid to the deck. She shut her eyes, and waited. After the screams stopped, worse sounds came. She wished she could cover her ears.

Finally, there was silence.

When she stopped shaking, she raised her hands to her mouth and worked on the knots.